Seaside Dream

BY *JANET COSTA BATES*

ILLUSTRATED BY **LAMBERT DAVIS**

Lee & Low Books Inc.

New York

GLOSSARY

Aura (AWR-uh): female name

Cape Verde (kayp vurd): country made up of a group of
  islands located off the west coast of Africa

kachupa (kuh-CHU-puh) *or* **munchupa** (mun-CHU-puh):
  national dish of Cape Verde; stew made of dried corn,
  dried beans, vegetables, and sometimes meat, which has
  many variations

mantenha (mahn-ten-YUH): greeting sent with people
  traveling between Cape Verde and the United States,
  essential for keeping relationships strong between family
  and friends separated by distance

Piedade (pee-uh-DAHD): female name

Text copyright © 2010 by Janet Costa Bates
Illustrations copyright © 2010 by Lambert Davis

LEE & LOW BOOKS Inc., 95 Madison Avenue, New York, NY 10016
leeandlow.com

Manufactured in China by Toppan, August 2010

Book design by Christy Hale
Book production by The Kids at Our House

The text is set in Cochin
The illustrations are rendered in acrylic

10 9 8 7 6 5 4 3 2 1
First Edition

Library of Congress Cataloging-in-Publication Data
Bates, Janet Costa.
Seaside dream / by Janet Costa Bates ; illustrated by Lambert Davis. — 1st ed.
    p. cm.
Summary: At a birthday celebration on the beach, Cora gives her grandmother a special
gift and encourages her to make a trip back to her home country, Cape Verde.
ISBN 978-1-60060-347-1 (hardcover : alk. paper)
[1. Grandmothers—Fiction. 2. Cape Verdean Americans—Fiction. 3. Birthdays—Fiction.
4. Gifts—Fiction.] I. Davis, Lambert, ill. II. Title.
PZ7.B316Se 2010
[E]—dc22   2009017049

To Maria Piedade Nobre Costa
Grandma, I love you still — J.C.B.

To journeys across the sea — L.D.

Cora couldn't remember the last time so many people had squeezed into Grandma's house. Joyful shouts filled the air, and there were hugs all around every time an aunt, an uncle, a cousin, or a friend walked through the doorway. Some hugs came with kisses. Some hugs came with hearty pats on the back. Some hugs even came with happy tears.

"Piedade," Uncle Manny greeted Grandma. "Tomorrow's the big day: your seventieth birthday! A once-in-a-lifetime thing."

Grandma smiled and reminded him, "Every birthday is a once-in-a-lifetime thing."

Family and friends had come from across the country and across town to celebrate Grandma's birthday. Cora felt she was the luckiest one of all. She came from right next door.

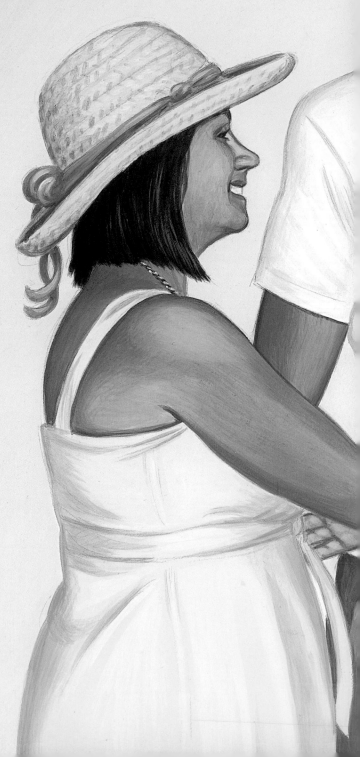

Cora and her cousin Gabe kept an eye on
the parade of presents coming into the house.
There were boxes of all sizes wrapped in colorful
paper and tied with ribbons and bows.

"I don't have a present for Grandma," Cora
whispered to Gabe.

"She doesn't care if you give her a present,"
he said.

"I know," said Cora. "But I care."

In no time the house was overflowing with stories, laughter, and food. Everyone was busy cooking for the big party the next day. Mostly they cooked Cape Verdean food since some family, like Grandma, had come to the United States from the Cape Verde Islands.

"Why is there so much food?" asked Cora.

"When your grandmother was still in Cape Verde, there wasn't always enough food," said Aunt Celia. "But now we are blessed with enough to share."

Uncle Manny dipped a spoon into a large pot and held it out to Cora for a taste.

"That's good *kachupa*, no?" he said.

"It's *MUNchupa*," Aunt Celia said of the stew.

"On my island we called it kachupa," insisted Uncle Manny.

"Well," said Aunt Celia. "You come from the wrong island!" Then they both laughed.

Cora and Gabe looked at each other and shrugged. Munchupa. Kachupa. It all tasted the same to them.

Cora liked being surrounded by family, but she missed having Grandma all to herself. She missed the walk on the beach she and Grandma took almost every day in the summer.

After dinner Cora left the noisy kitchen for the quiet back porch where she could watch the moonlight sparkle on the ocean. She tried to think of a birthday gift for Grandma. Cora was lost in thought when Grandma found her.

"I am thinking of taking a beach walk," said Grandma.

"But it's nighttime," said Cora. "It might be scary out there by yourself."

"Then maybe someone could come with me to hold my hand."

"Maybe someone could." Cora was happy to have Grandma all to herself again.

Grandma and Cora walked along the water's edge listening to the sea. Cora tossed a shell into the water and watched as the waves rocked it, carrying the small shell farther and farther away from the shore. Grandma stood silently looking out at the ocean.

"What's out there?" Cora asked Grandma.

"Aura, my sister. Across the ocean in the Old Country. The night before I left Cape Verde, there was a warm breeze just like tonight. We stood on the beach and made a promise that we would send each other as many *mantenhas* as there are stars."

"As many what?" Cora asked.

"Mantenhas. Messages. Sending a mantenha is like saying hello, but more. It means, though you are far away, I want to keep you in my life."

Uncle Manny always said Grandma had a smile so bright that it shone through her eyes. But now Cora saw sad eyes, not smiling ones. Cora wondered what it would feel like to be so far from someone you loved for so long.

"Why did you leave Cape Verde?" asked Cora.

"For a long time there was no rain on the islands, so no food would grow," Grandma said. "Many people were starving. I could not stay."

"Why didn't Aura come with you?"

"She said the islands were home. She could not make herself leave."

"You could visit Aura," Cora said as she and Grandma sat down on the sand.

"Almost forty years ago, I came here on a boat," Grandma said. "The journey was long and difficult, and I have not forgotten it. I will not do it again."

"You could take a plane. A plane would be fast," Cora told her.

Grandma shook her head.

"You made it across the ocean once," Cora said. "I know you could do it again."

The smile slowly slipped back into Grandma's eyes. She gave Cora a big hug and said, "My Cora, you have such faith."

That night as Cora lay in bed, she listened to the waves through the open window. The splashes and swooshes lulled her to sleep. Soon she began to fly the way you can fly only in a dream. Cora skimmed the tops of the waves, soaring across the ocean until she saw a beach.

On the beach was a woman standing tall and straight, with her silver-colored hair pulled back in a bun, just like Grandma's. Cora watched as the woman picked up a shell, gave it a kiss, and tossed it into the water.

From way up high, Cora watched as the ocean waves carried the shell farther and farther away from the shore.

The next morning Cora woke up knowing just what to give Grandma for her birthday. Cora would have to work quickly to finish her present before the party.

While everyone was busy getting ready for church, Cora got dressed and slipped outside. She gathered what she needed, then went back to her room and put everything together. Just as Cora was tying the ribbon on her gift she heard her mother call, "Cora, come on. Time to go."

After church it was time for Grandma's party. They all walked to the beach carrying plates and platters, bowls and pots brimming with food. Gabe looked very important carrying the birthday cake.

Uncle Manny struggled with a large stack of colorful presents.

"You drop the gifts, then no munchupa," Aunt Celia teased.

"KAchupa," Uncle Manny said, laughing.

Cora carried her own present that she had wrapped in a small paper bag.

They ate for what felt like hours and hours to Cora. At last it was time for Grandma to open her gifts. Everyone *oooh*ed and *aaah*ed when Grandma opened a big box containing a hat for church, then another with a hat for gardening. Someone even gave her a hat for the beach.

Cora wanted to give Grandma her present when they were alone. She waited while Grandma opened each gift slowly so as not to tear the paper. She watched as Grandma saved the ribbons and bows, gently putting each one aside. Cora almost couldn't stand it when Grandma stopped to give a big hug to the giver of each gift.

Once all the other presents had finally been opened, Cora tugged
on Grandma's arm.

"Please can we take our walk now?" Cora asked.

"My Cora, I would love to take our walk now," Grandma replied.

Cora held her gift carefully.

"Such a pretty bag," said Grandma. "What's inside?"

"You'll see." Cora was so excited, she felt as if she could fly right
up to the sky.

When they reached a quiet spot near the water, they sat down, and Cora handed Grandma her present. Grandma untied the ribbon and lifted out a small glass jar filled with sand and water. A few seashells and beach pebbles rested on top of the sand.

"How beautiful," said Grandma, admiring the jar. "Thank you, Cora."

"You know how the ocean brings everything back and forth?" said Cora. "I thought maybe Aura stood on this sand. Maybe she even picked up one of these shells."

Grandma's hands shook slightly as she took out a shell and touched it to her cheek.

"Grandma," Cora whispered. "I think Aura sent you a mantenha in my dream last night."

Grandma closed her eyes for a moment. When she opened them, she gazed out across the water.

"Cora," she said. "An airplane to Cape Verde—pretty fast, no?"

"Very fast," Cora replied.

Grandma turned to Cora. "I'm thinking maybe I could go visit."

"Would you go by yourself?" asked Cora.

"Maybe someone could come with me to hold my hand," said Grandma.

Cora's face lit up, a smile shining through her eyes. "Maybe someone could," she said.

Cape Verde is a small, tropical country made up of a cluster of islands located off the west coast of Africa. Cape Verdeans are a beautiful mix of mostly African and Portuguese ancestry. Their language is Cape Verdean Crioulo, a dialect of Portuguese with strong African influences. The islands were a colony of Portugal for about five hundred years before Cape Verde gained its independence on July 5, 1975.

Cape Verdeans have experienced severe droughts numerous times in their history. When the islands did not get any rain, food could not grow, and all too often people starved. A great number of Cape Verdeans, including all four of my grandparents, left the islands in search of a better life. Many of them came to the United States. Because of this migration, families were separated, sometimes forever. One way families stayed connected was through mantenhas. Traditionally, a mantenha is a verbal greeting sent with someone who is traveling between the United States and Cape Verde. In the early 1900s, traveling and communicating were difficult and expensive. Sending a mantenha was a way to keep the bonds of family and friendship strong.

In *Seaside Dream*, the beach setting and the plot details come from my imagination, but some of the characters in the story were inspired by real people. Cora's grandma is based on my own grandmother, Maria Piedade Nobre Costa. Born on the island of Santo Antão in 1899, my grandmother arrived in the United States on July 4, 1926. In America, she and my grandfather were able to make a home where there was always enough food to go around. Like Cora, I lived right next door to my grandmother and felt very lucky to spend a lot of time with her. She never made it back to her beloved homeland, but she always held Cape Verde close to her heart and shared many stories of the islands with me. Although this story is fictional, the love between grandparent and grandchild—the kind of love that Cora and her grandmother experience—was a very real part of my own story.